Gardening Tips

Collect fallen leaves. These will break down into compost, which will help plants grow.

Add vegetable scraps to the compost. Worms will break them down into plant food.

Save the seeds from your fruit and vegetables to plant next year.

Water plants regularly. There's no need to water them when it rains!

Guinea Pigs
Go Gardening

Kate Sheehy

Bob and Ginger loved to work in their garden.

Every winter the two guinea pigs decided what
they were going to grow the next year.

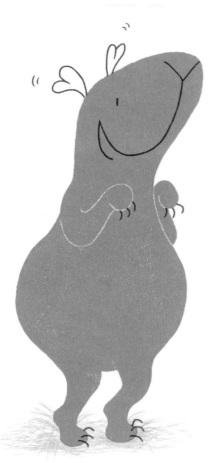

One dark night they began planning...

**"Let's plant strawberries.
I love strawberries!"**
said Bob.

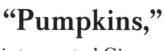

"Pumpkins,"
interrupted Ginger,
"they're my favourite."

Ginger wrote a list of all
the fruit and vegetables
they loved to eat.

The list kept getting longer...
and longer...and longer!

Strawberries
Peppers
Lettuces
TURNIPS
Radishes
Pumpkins
Spinach
Aubergines
CARROTS
Peas

Spring had finally sprung and the best friends
couldn't wait to get started.

Apple tree

Garden shed

watering
hose

Watering can

Trowel

Flower pots

Bob and Ginger's first job
was to prepare healthy soil for
their plants to grow in.

"First we better get rid of these weeds to make room for our plants," said Ginger.

Fork

Compost bin

Lawn mower

Rake

Shovel

Bob and Ginger began work battling the weeds.

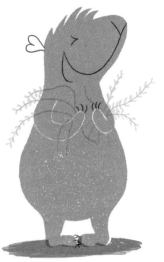

It was hard work
but very satisfying.

Their favourite weeds
were dandelions.

Dandelion leaves
are a tasty treat for
guinea pigs!

After weeding, Bob raked the soil to remove stones and Ginger gently turned the soil over to soften it.

"Now we are ready to add our compost to the soil," cheered Ginger.

compost makes the soil rich and healthy.

Bob and Ginger make their compost in a special bin at the end of the garden.

They add fallen leaves, straw, vegetable scraps, and cut grass to the bin, as well as used cardboard and newspaper.

Over time it breaks down into brown, crumbly soil that is perfect to help plants grow!

"This compost will help us grow **ginormous plants!**"
exclaimed Bob.

Ginger carefully mixed
the compost into
the soil.

It was now time for Bob and Ginger
to start planting.

"But where on earth are we going to plant everything?" thought Bob.

It was important that their vegetables had space to grow.

So Ginger measured out a row big enough
for every plant.

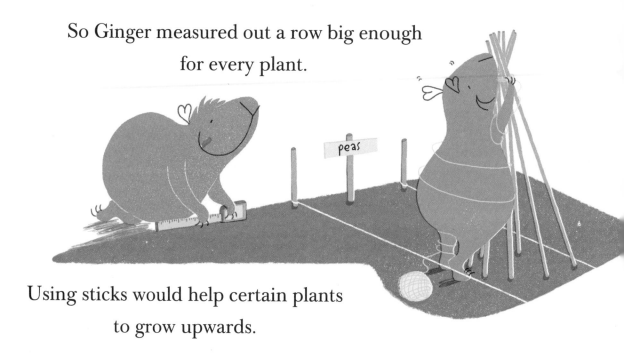

Using sticks would help certain plants
to grow upwards.

They sowed seeds in shallow holes and covered them with a little soil.
Then they gave them a sprinkling of water.

Bob and Ginger made sure that their plants would get plenty of sunlight.

Plants use light to make their own food.

"This sunny spot is perfect for our strawberries," smiled Bob.

"Let's plant our tomatoes here too," said Ginger. "They will grow **big and red and juicy!**"

While sowing seeds Bob found lots of wriggly worms.

"Ginger, look!" he shouted.

Bob and Ginger get super excited when they find earthworms.

Worms move through the soil
making tunnels. These tunnels
allow air and water to flow to the
seeds and roots of a plant.

Plants need air and water to grow.

After planting, Ginger drew a big chart on their blackboard
so that they would know when to harvest everything.

EARLY SUMMER

SUMMER

Lettuce

spinach

strawberries

Radishes

Tomatoes

SPRING ONIONS

CABBAGE

Peppers

Cucumbers

TURNIP

Carrots

Peas

"**Great,**" thought Bob, "**everything is going to plan. Nothing can possibly go wrong...**"

Except it did...

"G-g-g-ingerrrr..."

Bob said anxiously.

"Something's been eating our plants."

"Oh nooooo," cried Ginger.

"And the weeds have grown back too," she added.

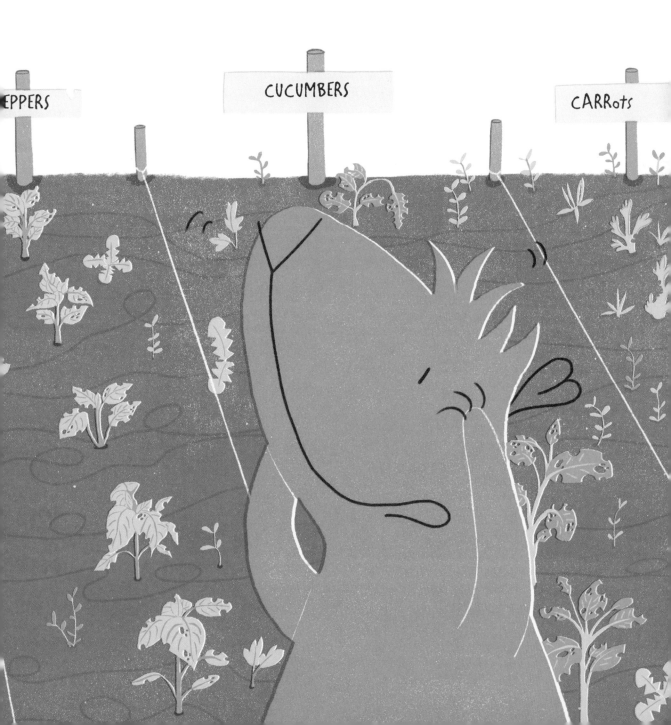

That night, Bob and Ginger took their torch and went out
in search of the leaf-munching culprits.

Bob gasped. There were slimy slugs on all of the leaves.

"Quick Bob, get them off!" squealed Ginger.

While they had a hard time keeping the slugs away, Bob and Ginger
had more luck with the weed problem.

They put straw around the plants to stop weeds from growing.

"Problem solved!" said Bob, though a little too soon...

They also had pesky pigeons trying to nibble their strawberries!

They covered the strawberries with
netting so the pigeons couldn't
get to them.

Fortunately, Bob and Ginger did not
have to fight off every creature...

They welcomed lots of buzzy bees to their garden!

Bees move powdery pollen from flower to flower, which is a process called pollination. After pollination, plants can produce seeds that grow into delicious fruit and vegetables.

Bob and Ginger took a well-earned break while the bees got to work.

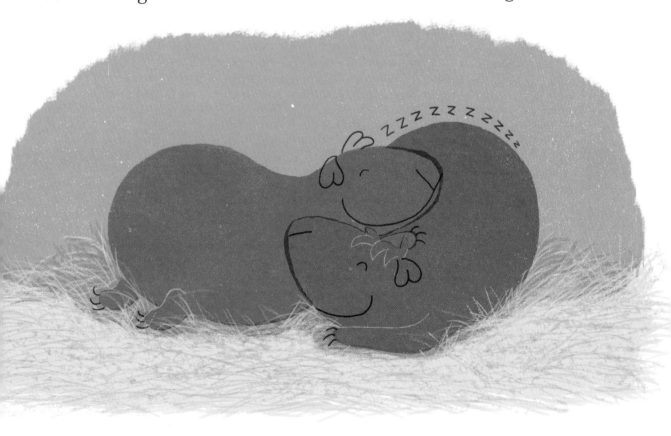

Then finally one day the first of their crops were ready.

"Ginger, look at all of these radishes!" shouted Bob.

"Our lettuce and spinach are ready too," smiled Ginger.

"Tomatoes, yummy!" chuckled Ginger.

"Mmmm...these are the juiciest strawberries I have ever tasted," mumbled Bob with his mouth full.

Ginger cleaned the
fresh vegetables
before making a
crunchy salad.

"Yum, yum!"
said Bob, reaching for
the leaves.

**"Bob, wait until
it's ready,"**
scolded Ginger.

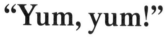

Compost

Bob used the strawberries to make a scrumptious jam.

He filled enough jars to last the whole year!

Later that summer Bob dug up
turnips and carrots.

Ginger picked peas, peppers,
cucumbers, and cabbages.

Then in autumn came
aubergines, sweetcorn...

... and tonnes of apples
from their apple trees.

There were also plenty of huge pumpkins
and watermelons.

"We will have tasty
meals for months,"
said Ginger
cheerfully!

After all of their hard work Bob and Ginger sat down to enjoy
a slice of their delicious homemade apple pie.

We make a great gardening team, don't we Bob?" boasted Ginger.

"Mmmhmm," agreed Bob.

Then it was time to start planning for next year...

 Penguin Random House

DK LONDON
Acquisitions Editor Sam Priddy
Senior Commissioning Designer Joanne Clark
Designer Eleanor Bates
Additional Editorial Abi Luscombe
Production Editor Dragana Puvacic
Production Controller John Casey
Jacket Co-ordinator Issy Walsh
Publishing Manager Francesca Young
Publishing Director Sarah Larter

First published in Great Britain in 2020 by
Dorling Kindersley Limited
One Embassy Gardens, 8 Viaduct Gardens,
London, SW11 7AY

Imported into the EEA by Dorling Kindersley Verlag GmbH.
Arnulfstr. 124, 80636 Munich, Germany

Copyright © 2020 Dorling Kindersley Limited
A Penguin Random House Company
10 9 8 7 6 5 4 3 2 1
001–320596-Feb/2020

A CIP catalogue record for this book
is available from the British Library.
ISBN: 978-0-2414-5310-0

Printed and bound in China

For the curious
www.dk.com

MIX
Paper from
responsible sources
FSC™ C018179